Pokémon

ALOLA REGION ADVENTURE GUIDE

BY SONIA SANDER AND SIMCHA WHITEHILL

SCHOLASTIC INC.

All rights reserved. Published by Scholastic Inc., *Publishers since 1920.* SCHOLASTIC and associated logos are trademarks and/or registered trademarks of Scholastic Inc.

The publisher does not have any control over and does not assume any responsibility for author or third-party websites or their content.

No part of this publication may be reproduced, stored in a retrieval system, or transmitted in any form or by any means, electronic, mechanical, photocopying, recording, or otherwise, without written permission of the publisher. For information regarding permission, write to Scholastic Inc., Attention: Permissions Department, 557 Broadway, New York, NY 10012.

This book is a work of fiction. Names, characters, places, and incidents are either the product of the author's imagination or are used fictitiously, and any resemblance to actual persons, living or dead, business establishments, events, or locales is entirely coincidental.

ISBN 978-1-338-14860-2

10 9 8 7 6 5 4 3 2 1   18 19 20 21 22

Printed in the U.S.A.   40
First printing 2018

CONTENTS

ALOLA TO NEW ADVENTURE

What starts as a vacation in the Alola region turns into an amazing new adventure in Ash Ketchum's quest to become a Pokémon Master! There's so much for Ash and his best buddy, Pikachu, to explore as they travel around this sunny new region and meet the friendly people and Pokémon that call Alola home.

The many islands of Alola are truly an oasis for their peaceful inhabitants. There is a real sense of togetherness between humans and Pokémon here. And Alola has so many natural wonders to explore! To get around the islands, humans rely on Pokémon to go anywhere and everywhere. They refer to these traveling Pokémon as Ride Pokémon.

If you're traveling on land, look for a Land Ride Pokémon or a Pokémon Taxi like this one powered by Tauros.

When you want to fly, hop on board an Air Ride Pokémon like Pelipper.

If there's a lake, river, ocean, or stream to cross, sail over with a Water Ride Pokémon like Sharpedo.

ASH AND PIKACHU

Ash and his amazing Electric-type Pokémon pal, Pikachu, have been together from the very beginning. They have traveled far and wide and tackled countless adventures. Together, they are an unstoppable team!

The two friends' latest journey takes them a long, long way from their home of Pallet Town in the Kanto region. After training hard, they've decided to play hard and have a little fun in the sun on Melemele Island in the Alola region.

Ash soon meets cool Professor Kukui, fun-loving Principal Samson Oak, and five new Pokémon Trainer friends from the local Pokémon School—Kiawe, Lana, Mallow, Sophocles, and Lillie.

But Ash's old foes have followed him to the new region. Team Rocket has also made the trip to the islands, and they're looking to swipe some high-powered Pokémon. In Alola, they have some evil competition—Team Skull, a group of misfits who love to cause chaos.

WELCOME TO ALOLA!

Alola is made up of four islands: Melemele, Akala, Poni, and Ula'ula. There are many native Pokémon that have existed in Alola for generations as well as Pokémon that have come to the island paradise from other regions.

Ash starts his Alolan adventure right on Melemele Island. Some lucky students get to attend the local Pokémon School on the shore. Now those are classrooms with a view!

Akala Island is home to the Wela Volcano. Ash first visits the island when he helps his buddy Kiawe deliver Moomoo Milk from his family's farm on Akala.

ALOLA'S FIRST PARTNER POKÉMON

ROWLET
The Grass Quill Pokémon

How to Say It: ROW-let
("ROW" rhymes with "NOW")
Height: 1'00"
Weight: 3.3 lbs.
Type: Grass-Flying

During the day, Rowlet rests and generates energy via photosynthesis. In the night, it flies silently to sneak up on foes and launch a flurry of kicking attacks.

EVOLUTION

Rowlet   Dartrix   Decidueye

LITTEN

The Fire Cat Pokémon

How to Say It: LIT-n
Height: 1'04"
Weight: 9.5 lbs.
Type: Fire

When it grooms its fur, Litten is storing up ammunition—the flaming fur is later coughed up in a fiery attack. Trainers often have a hard time getting this solitary Pokémon to trust them.

EVOLUTION

Litten   Torracat   Incineroar

POPPLIO

The Sea Lion Pokémon

How to Say It: POP-lee-oh
Height: 1'04"
Weight: 16.5 lbs.
Type: Water

Popplio uses the water balloons it blows from its nose as a weapon in battle. It's a hard worker and puts in lots of practice creating and controlling these balloons.

EVOLUTION

Popplio   Brionne   Primarina

ROTOM DEX

Professor Kukui gives Ash an amazing gift to help him get started in the Alola region. It's an unusual Pokédex that's inhabited by the Pokémon Rotom—a Rotom Dex! This handy electronic device is packed with information on the known species of Pokémon. It can recognize any Pokémon in a flash, so Rotom Dex sure comes in handy as Ash explores Alola.

ASH'S POKÉMON IN ALOLA

ROWLET

Ash happily shares his lunch with a wild Pokémon he meets, a very hungry Rowlet. After the meal, Ash follows Rowlet to meet its Pikipek pals—and they arrive just in the nick of time! Tricky Team Rocket is trying to catch all the Pikipek in their net. Ash and Pikachu snap into action and battle Team Rocket back so Rowlet has a chance to free its friends.

With help from Bewear, Team Rocket is sent blasting off again. But Rowlet won't let Ash go anywhere until he offers to take it along, too! So Ash tosses a Poké Ball and catches his new Pokémon pal.

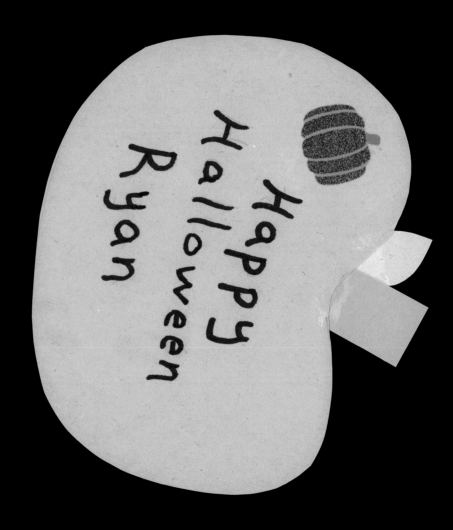

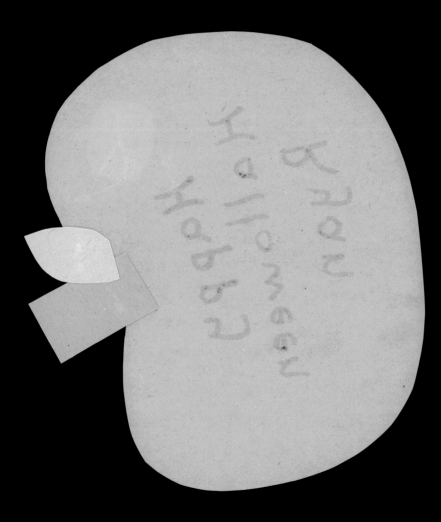

ROCKRUFF

When Ash and Professor Kukui spot a wild Rockruff limping home, covered in scratches and burns, they're determined to find out what happened. The next night, they sneak out to follow Rockruff to Clawmark Hill, where two Lycanroc keep watch over the wild Pokémon who come together to battle and train.

They watch as Rockruff bravely battles a fearsome Magmar, but it is defeated. So Ash offers to help it learn a new bold move with a boulder—Rock Throw. After some serious training with Ash and Pikachu, Rockruff returns to challenge Magmar to a rematch—and this time, it wins!

After seeing how well Ash and Rockruff work together, Professor Kukui thinks Ash would be the perfect Pokémon Trainer for it. Both Pikachu and Rockruff agree! So Ash tosses his Poké Ball and catches his newest champion chum, Rockruff.

ASH'S ARRIVAL IN ALOLA

Ash raced across the sea on the back of Sharpedo. "Yippee!" he shouted. "This is AWESOME!! Right, Pikachu?"

"*Piiiika-chuuuuuuuu!*" the bright yellow Electric Pokémon replied.

Ash couldn't have imagined a better beginning to his vacation on Melemele Island. He was really enjoying the ride with his best friend, Pikachu, by his side.

Ash and Pikachu took a great big breath and held on tight as Sharpedo dove down deep into the crystal blue water. There were so many species of Water-type Pokémon swimming under the sea! He almost hated to head back toward shore.

Back at the hotel, Ash checked in with his mom and Mr. Mime, who were relaxing poolside.

"Hey, Mom! I'm back," he called.

"I hope you had fun, Ash," she said.

"I sure did!" Ash replied, launching into a full report of his ride.

"We have Mimey to thank for winning the tickets for our Alola vacation," said his mom. "So! Shall we change and get going?"

"Where to, Mom?" wondered Ash.

"Why, to Professor Oak's cousin's place," she answered.

Ash was having so much fun in the sun he had almost forgotten that Professor Oak had asked Ash and his mom to make a delivery for him—a very special Pokémon Egg.

On the way, Ash, his mom, and Mr. Mime traveled by Pokémon Taxi—pulled by Tauros.

"This is the best ever!" Ash cheered.

"Here in the Alola region, we use the power of Pokémon to go anywhere and everywhere. We refer to these Pokémon as Ride Pokémon," said their driver. "When you travel on land, you take a Land Ride Pokémon. When you want to fly, you take an Air Ride Pokémon. On water, a Water Ride Pokémon."

Ash was fascinated. "So that Sharpedo was a Water Ride Pokémon!"

Their driver could see that Ash was already getting the lay of the land in Alola. And they were about to explore another amazing spot in the region.

"Mom, where are we taking the Egg?" Ash asked.

"To a place they call the Pokémon School," she said.

Now she had Ash's full attention!

But not for long. Just then Mr. Mime pointed out a roadside berry stand. While Ash's mom stopped to buy some berries, Ash had a bit of a surprise. A Grubbin popped out of the ground right in front of him . . . and grabbed him by the nose with its giant jaws!

As Ash fell to his knees, clutching his nose in pain, Grubbin dove back into the ground and took off, leaving behind a trail of dirt. After feeling Grubbin's strength firsthand, Ash was impressed by the wild Bug-type with bite.

"Okay, let's catch it, Pikachu!" said Ash. He sprang back into action and charged off after the Pokémon.

Grubbin led Ash up the street and into the dark woods, where two bright, glowing Pokémon eyes followed Ash's every movement. It was the watchful guardian of Melemele Island, Tapu Koko! The Legendary Pokémon swooped through the treetops above as Ash dove to catch Grubbin.

But Grubbin was too quick. It slipped away. As Ash began digging after the wild Pokémon, Grubbin burrowed even deeper into the ground.

Suddenly, Ash and Pikachu heard a distant sound and stopped in their tracks. A few moments later, a very large Bewear stumbled across their path.

"Oh, wow! Look, it's waving," cried Ash. "You sure are cute!"

But Ash's reaction quickly turned to fear as Bewear roared loudly and began swinging its mighty paws.

"Move it!" screamed Ash as he and Pikachu ran for safety.

As soon as Ash and Pikachu were clear of Bewear, the young Trainer spotted something blasting across the blue sky.

"A Charizard?" exclaimed Ash. "Must be an Air Ride Pokémon. That's awesome! Pikachu, let's follow it!"

Pikachu jumped up onto Ash's shoulder, and Ash took off running. In no time at all, they were out of the forest. Before them was a group of large buildings surrounded by a bright blue moat and beautiful grounds filled with people and Pokémon.

Ash was so distracted by the scene that he didn't notice the three Tauros speeding down the path toward him.

Lillie, a girl in a big white hat with long blond hair, tried to warn Ash, but it was too late. The racing Tauros knocked Ash over!

The three young riders quickly stopped and dismounted.

Luckily, Ash wasn't hurt. He hopped up and quickly dusted himself off.

"I'm Ash Ketchum. I came from Pallet Town in the Kanto region! And this is my good buddy Pikachu," Ash introduced himself. "What is this place?"

One of the riders, Mallow, a girl with long bright green hair and a Bounsweet on her shoulder, told Ash it was the Pokémon School. She offered to show Ash around.

"This is great!" exclaimed Ash as they entered a room full of prehistoric Pokémon skeletons. He couldn't believe his eyes!

Next, Mallow took Ash to the principal's office, where as luck would have it, Ash's mom was waiting with Mr. Mime and the Pokémon Egg.

"Alola, Ash!" said the principal. "Welcome to the Pokémon School, home of Solrock and roll!"

"Professor Oak, what are you doing here?" asked Ash.

The principal laughed. "People tell me we look alike. I guess that's why you recognize me. The name is Samson Oak. Nice to meet 'chu."

"He always makes jokes, playing around with Pokémon names," Mallow whispered.

Mallow offered to show Ash around the rest of the campus. Along the way, she introduced Ash to Professor Kukui.

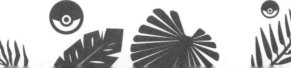

"I hope you enjoy your visit here!" said Professor Kukui.

Ash was suddenly distracted. Down below, on the ground, three troublemakers dressed in skull T-shirts got off their bikes and started bothering a boy named Kiawe and his Charizard.

"Who are those guys?" Ash asked Mallow.

"They're part of Team Skull," Mallow explained. "They're constantly bullying us and trying to pick a fight."

Team Skull was doing exactly that. Ash, Mallow, and Professor Kukui hurried down to the battle that was unfolding.

Team Skull called out their Pokémon—Salandit, Yungoos, and Zubat.

"Now tell your Charizard to fight," demanded Team Skull's leader.

But before Kiawe could respond, Ash jumped in. "Stop it! You're cowards, ganging up three against one!"

"What are you gonna do about it?" asked the Team Skull leader.

"I'll fight, too!" Ash replied. "Are you ready?"

Although Kiawe was reluctant to drag Ash into the battle, Ash and Pikachu were prepared to fight! Kiawe and Ash battled back with Pikachu and the Blast Turtle Pokémon, Turtonator. Together they kept Team Skull on their toes.

Then Kiawe stepped up with a special attack called a Z-Move that Ash had never seen before. As Kiawe moved his arms and spun around, a golden ray of

light blasted from the Z-Ring on his arm, and a glow engulfed his whole body.

"The zenith of my mind, of body, and spirit! Like the great mountain of Akala, become a raging fire and burn! Inferno Overdrive!" exclaimed Kiawe.

Kiawe hurled the fiery energy to Turtonator, who exploded with red-hot power. Team Skull's Pokémon were left in a smoldering crater on the ground.

As Team Skull retreated in defeat, Ash wanted to know more about Kiawe's unbelievable final move.

"Only those who participate in a ceremony called the Island Challenge are able to use Z-Moves," explained Professor Kukui.

Since coming to Alola, Ash had encountered so many incredible things—Island Guardians, an Island Challenge, and now Z-Moves, too! More than anything in the world, Ash wanted to remain in Alola after his vacation. Professor Kukui kindly offered to let Ash stay at his house while he attended the Pokémon School.

And so, what began as a short vacation turned in to the promise of many, many exciting adventures to come in the Alola region!

THE POKÉMON SCHOOL

The Pokémon School is located on a big, beautiful campus where students work with Pokémon and learn alongside them. Ash was fascinated by the school from the first moment he stepped onto its lush green grounds. It is here that he learns all about the Alola region, Z-Rings, Tapu Koko, the Island Challenge, the difference between Pokémon and Alolan Pokémon, and much, much more.

This is one cool school that Pokémon and Pokémon fans flock to because they know knowledge is truly power!

The grounds of Alola's Pokémon School

Ash and Mallow check out the fossils of prehistoric Pokémon.

A typical classroom

PRINCIPAL SAMSON OAK

When Ash first meets Samson Oak, he thinks he's found a familiar face in Alola, but he's really just a relative of one. Samson Oak is the cousin of the famous Professor Oak of Kanto and he is the principal of the Pokémon School.

The resemblance between the two cousins goes way beyond looks. Samson Oak shares a love of science and Pokémon with his cousin. Samson Oak's area of research is regional variants of Pokémon, such as Alolan Exeggutor.

For someone who studies something so serious, Samson Oak is a really easygoing guy with a silly sense of humor. The principal can't resist making puns out of Pokémon names—what about 'chu?

KOMALA

Principal Samson Oak's best Pokémon pal is Komala.

Komala never wakes up—ever—although it does sometimes move around as it dreams. It lives in a permanent state of sleep, cuddling its precious log or its Trainer's arm.

PROFESSOR KUKUI

Professor Kukui is a favorite teacher among the students at the Pokémon School. He invited Ash to stay at his home in Alola so that he could attend the special school.

Professor Kukui's area of expertise is Pokémon moves—he likes to sneak Pokémon attack names into his everyday conversations. You won't find this sporty schoolteacher spending all his time inside a lab. Professor Kukui loves to get hands-on experience in the great outdoors.

KIAWE

Some people take a bus to school, but Kiawe has a much cooler ride—his best buddy, Charizard. They do everything together, including delivering milk from his family's farm.

Kiawe didn't catch Charizard—the Flame Pokémon was passed down from his grandfather. But Kiawe isn't the kind of guy who easily accepts gifts or help. He is headstrong and proud, which can sometimes make him seem grumpy. He works hard for what he has—and that includes the Z-Ring given to him by Kahuna Olivia of Akala Island.

TURTONATOR

Kiawe travels around with two Pokémon pals, Charizard and Turtonator.

Poisonous gases and flames spew from Turtonator's nostrils. Its shell is made of unstable material that might explode upon impact, so opponents are advised to aim for its stomach instead.

LANA

Lana is one of Ash's classmates, but she's not the kind of student who's always raising her hand. Lana struggles to find words to express what she's thinking and feeling, but she's by no means a pushover. In fact, Lana can be quite stubborn, and she likes to get her own way. This can be a challenge since Lana lives with her grandmother, parents, twin younger sisters, and a bunch of fishermen. Even if Lana wanted to talk, how would she ever get a word in edgewise?

POPPLIO

Popplio uses the water balloons it blows from its nose as a weapon in battle. It's a hard worker and puts in lots of practice creating and controlling these balloons.

When Ash's class went on a fishing trip, Professor Kukui put Lana in charge. Everyone was surprised when Team Rocket showed up and scooped up all their Pokémon in a net. Then Team Rocket dropped the Pokémon toward some rocks! Fortunately, Lana's Popplio quickly created a giant water balloon to cushion the fall and save the day!

MALLOW

Mallow is a ball of energy! She runs on instinct and isn't afraid to dive into any situation, but she occasionally jumps to conclusions. In fact, Mallow loves all kinds of jumping—both in her mind and on the field. One of her favorite things to do is play sports. She's also a very good cook and often helps out at the local restaurant, where she lives with her brother and father.

Mallow has a lot to give, and she never gives up. She is very protective of her good friends Lana and Lillie. When she cares about something, she gives it her all.

BOUNSWEET

Bounsweet smells good enough to eat—which sometimes gets it into trouble! The intensely sugary liquid it gives off can be diluted to bring the sweetness level down so people can drink it.

Bounsweet is the perfect Pokémon for a Trainer like Mallow who loves to cook. When Mallow wanted to make the famous Alolan stew, Ash offered to help her track down a missing ingredient, Yellow Nectar. Using Bounsweet's irresistible sugary scent, they lured the Yellow Nectar–loving Oricorio. When tricky Team Rocket seized the moment to set a trap, Bounsweet quickly stepped in to battle back the terrible trio and save its pals.

SOPHOCLES

Sophocles acts like a slacker, but he's actually really motivated to learn about technology. A computer programming whiz, he's obsessed with how the Rotom Pokédex works and has even taken one apart to get a closer look.

Sophocles can explain even the most complex things about tech, but otherwise, he might come off as a nervous wreck. He is a sensitive soul who relates better to machines than he does to people.

TOGEDEMARU

Its back is covered with long, spiny fur that usually lies flat. Togedemaru can bristle up the fur during battle for use as a weapon, or during storms to attract lightning, which it stores as electricity in its body.

Togedemaru is the perfect Pokémon for Sophocles. One day, when Ash and Sophocles were at the mall together, Team Rocket sent the building's security system into complete shutdown. Sophocles snapped into action and used his computer programming skills to bring it all back online. Then he called on Togedemaru to team up with Ash, Rowlet, and Pikachu. Together, they took care of that tricky trio Team Rocket!

LILLIE

Lillie's family is wealthy—her butler drives her to school every day! Some might think she's a total snob, but, in fact, Lillie is one of the kindest kids at the Pokémon School. And she's also one of the hardest-working students.

Lillie wants to learn all she can about Pokémon . . . but would you believe that for a long time, she didn't like touching them? Fortunately, all that changed once she met her best Pokémon buddy, Alolan Vulpix.

ALOLAN VULPIX

Vulpix in the Alola region were once known as Keokeo, and some older folks still use that name. Its six tails can create a spray of ice crystals to cool itself off when it gets too hot.

When Principal Oak tasked Ash's class with taking care of a Pokémon Egg, someone had to volunteer to bring it home with them after school. To help Lillie get over her fear of touching Pokémon, Mallow suggested she be responsible for the Egg. At first, Lillie was nervous. But when a hungry Salandit went after the Egg, she threw her arms around the Egg to protect it. It later hatched and revealed an Alolan Vulpix!

NURSE JOY

If your Pokémon is injured, sick, or just plain tired, it will receive excellent care from Nurse Joy at the Pokémon Center. Nurse Joy relies on her attentive Pokémon pals to help with all her patients.

OFFICER JENNY

If you spot an evildoer lurking around town, be sure to call on the best crime-stopper in the biz: Officer Jenny. Since there is strength in numbers, she often has a Pokémon pal by her side.

TEAM ROCKET

Like Ash, Jessie, James, and Meowth of Team Rocket are first-time visitors to Alola. Their trip got off to a bumpy start when the first Pokémon they met was a mysterious Mimikyu that drew Meowth into a nightmare! But once Ash and his classmates happened upon the scene, Mimikyu decided to battle on Team Rocket's side. The battle was cut short by a big Bewear who grabbed Jessie and James and carried them off.

Don't fret for the tricky trio, though—they're living in an Alolan dream ever since. Wild Bewear has been treating them to a nonstop banquet of delicious berries and honey!

™

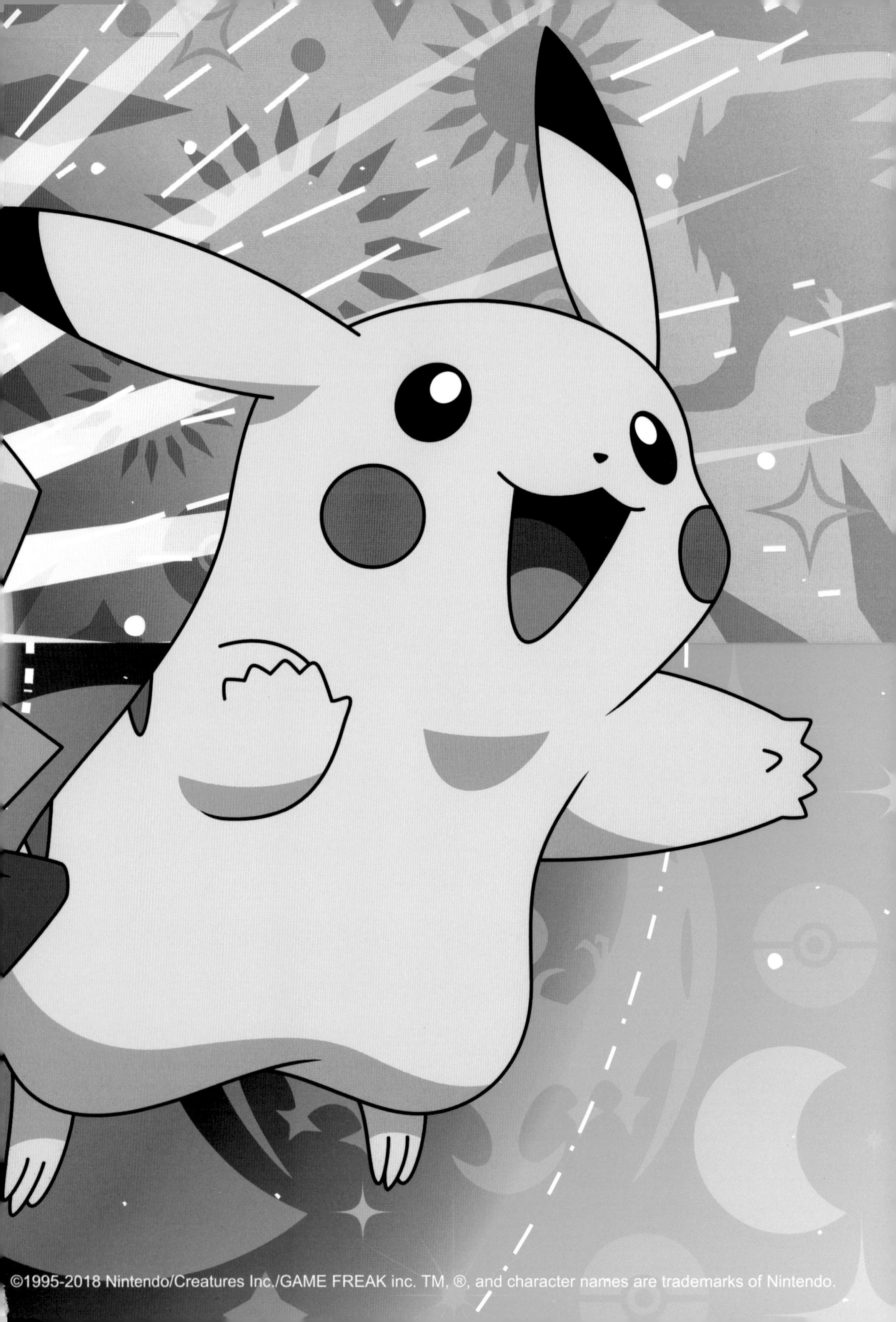

BEWEAR

Think twice before making friends with a Bewear. This super-strong Pokémon might be even more dangerous to those it likes because it tends to deliver bone-crushing hugs as a sign of affection. Beware!

MIMIKYU

What does Mimikyu look like? No one really knows, but apparently it's terrifying—it always hides underneath an old rag so it doesn't scare anyone while it's trying to make friends.

TEAM SKULL

In the Alola region, a group of bullies known as Team Skull are bad to the bone. They have made it their mission to cause a lot of trouble. They like to talk tough and steal other people's Pokémon.

Ash first encountered Team Skull trying to battle Kiawe three against one on the Pokémon School grounds. Ash hadn't met Kiawe yet, but it didn't matter. He was right there by his side to stand up against Team Skull. Ash called them out for being bullies and cowards. Then he called on his pal Pikachu to help Kiawe and Turtonator defeat the terrible trio.

Ash came face-to-face with Team Skull a second time on Akala Island while he and Kiawe were attempting to deliver ingredients to a local baker. Team Skull wanted payback for the last battle and threatened to steal the cargo. But Ash and Pikachu managed to chase them off with the electrifying Z-Move Gigavolt Havoc.

POKÉMON VS. ALOLA POKÉMON

In Alola, Ash encounters some Pokémon that make him do a double take. They sure look like Pokémon he's met, but something has changed. At first, Ash wasn't able to put his finger on it, but with a little research, Ash discovers that the Alolan Pokémon can look similar to Pokémon species he's familiar with, but, in fact, they can be very different and possibly even be a different type.

According to Professor Samson Oak, some Pokémon can develop a distinct appearance based on the region in which they live. For example, the reason Alolan Exeggutor have grown taller is Alola's year-round warm and sunny climate. Some believe that an Alolan Exeggutor looks exactly the way it's supposed to thanks to living in this ideal environment.

DIGLETT

Height: 0'08"
Weight: 1.8 lbs.
Type: Ground

To farmers, Diglett can be a blessing or a curse! The soil it lives in becomes rich and fertile, great for growing crops—but this Pokémon can also be destructive, chewing on the roots of those crops.

ALOLAN DIGLETT

Height: 0'08"
Weight: 2.2 lbs.
Type: Ground-Steel

The metal hairs that sprout from the top of Diglett's head can be used to communicate or to sense its surroundings. It can extend just those hairs aboveground to make sure everything is safe before emerging.

DUGTRIO

Height: 2'04"
Weight: 73.4 lbs.
Type: Ground

By working together, the triplets that make up a Dugtrio can dig sixty miles into the ground. No one knows what this Pokémon's body looks like, because only its heads show above the dirt.

ALOLAN DUGTRIO

Height: 2'04"
Weight: 146.8 lbs.
Type: Ground-Steel

Although Dugtrio's golden hair is shiny and beautiful, people aren't inclined to collect it when it falls—there are stories that doing so will bring bad luck. In Alola, this Pokémon is thought to represent the spirit of the land.

EXEGGUTOR

Height: 6'07"
Weight: 264.6 lbs.
Type: Grass-Psychic

Exeggutor's three heads all have minds of their own, and every decision involves a telepathic discussion. Sometimes one of the heads drops to the ground and grows into an Exeggcute.

ALOLAN EXEGGUTOR

Height: 35'09"
Weight: 916.2 lbs.
Type: Grass-Dragon

In the tropical sun and sand, Exeggutor grows exceptionally tall, unlocking draconic powers hidden deep within. Trainers in Alola are proud of the tree-like Exeggutor and consider this to be its ideal form.

GEODUDE

Height: 1'04"
Weight: 44.1 lbs.
Type: Rock-Ground

It might be tempting to gather up Geodude found along the road and throw them around like balls, but that's a bad idea—they're very heavy, and their surface is extremely hard. Ouch!

GOLEM

Height: 4'07"
Weight: 661.4 lbs.
Type: Rock-Ground

Golem's annual molt leaves behind a shell that makes for good fertilizer when incorporated into the soil. This Pokémon can easily stand up to an explosion, but it really hates getting wet.

ALOLAN GEODUDE

Height: 1'04"
Weight: 44.8 lbs.
Type: Rock-Electric

In the Alola region, Geodude are naturally magnetic, and their bodies are often covered in iron particles they've picked up while sleeping in the sand. Stepping on one can cause a nasty shock, so beachgoers keep a sharp eye out.

ALOLAN GOLEM

Height: 5'07"
Weight: 696.7 lbs.
Type: Rock-Electric

The rocks Golem fires from its back carry a strong electrical charge, so even a glancing blow can deliver a powerful shock. Sometimes it grabs a Geodude to fire instead.

GRAVELER

Height: 3'03"
Weight: 231.5 lbs.
Type: Rock-Ground

Graveler can't walk very fast, but when it tucks itself into a ball, it can roll as fast as a car once it gains momentum. It loves to crunch on moss-covered rocks.

ALOLAN GRAVELER

Height: 3'03"
Weight: 242.5 lbs.
Type: Rock-Electric

The crystals that appear on Graveler's body are the result of consuming dravite, a particularly tasty mineral. Graveler often fight over dravite deposits, crashing together with a sound like thunder.

GRIMER

Height: 2'11"
Weight: 66.1 lbs.
Type: Poison

Most people and
Pokémon dislike
the industrial
waste created by
factories, but
Grimer happily
feasts on the
icky slime.
To survive,
it has to
maintain a certain
level of germs in its body.

MAROWAK

Height: 3'03"
Weight: 99.2 lbs.
Type: Ground

Evolution has
transformed this
formerly weak and
frightened Pokémon
into a fearsome foe.
Marowak uses bones
as projectile weapons
against those it
considers enemies.

ALOLAN GRIMER

Height: 2'04"
Weight: 92.6 lbs.
Type: Poison-Dark

Grimer's appearance in the Alola
region developed after it was called
upon to deal with a persistent
garbage problem. Each crystal
on its body is formed
from dangerous
toxins, and
those toxins
escape if a
crystal falls off.

ALOLAN
MAROWAK

Height: 3'03"
Weight: 75.0 lbs.
Type: Fire-Ghost

The flaming bone that
Marowak spins like a
baton once belonged
to its mother, and
it's protected by its
mother's spirit. It
grieves for its fallen
companions, visiting
their graves along the
roadside.

MEOWTH
Height: 1'04"
Weight: 9.3 lbs.
Type: Normal

Meowth lazes about during the day and becomes active at night, when it roams city streets looking for coins and other shiny objects. It has developed a rivalry with Murkrow.

ALOLAN MEOWTH
Height: 1'04"
Weight: 9.3 lbs.
Type: Dark

Meowth is very vain about the golden Charm on its forehead, becoming enraged if any dirt dulls its bright surface. These crafty Pokémon are not native to Alola, but thanks to human interference, their population has surged.

MUK

Height: 3'11"
Weight: 66.1 lbs.
Type: Poison

Muk really stinks, but some Trainers are fond of it, terrible smell and all. Recent efforts to reduce pollution and clean up the environment have also reduced this Pokémon's numbers.

NINETALES

Height: 3'07"
Weight: 43.9 lbs.
Type: Fire

Ninetales is capable of bending fire to its will. It can live for a thousand years and was created when nine saints merged into a single being, according to legend.

ALOLAN MUK

Height: 3'03"
Weight: 114.6 lbs.
Type: Poison-Dark

Muk's bright and colorful markings are the result of chemical changes in its body, caused by its diet of all sorts of garbage. It's generally a pleasant and friendly companion, but if it gets hungry, it can turn destructive.

ALOLAN NINETALES

Height: 3'07"
Weight: 43.9 lbs.
Type: Ice-Fairy

In its frosty coat, Ninetales creates ice droplets that can be used to shower over opponents. It's generally calm and collected, but if it becomes angry, it can freeze the offenders in their tracks.

PERSIAN
Height: 3'03"
Weight: 70.5 lbs.
Type: Normal

It's tough to become friends with this Pokémon. Persian is vain and violent, and anyone who meets its gaze will feel the pain of its sharp claws.

ALOLAN PERSIAN
Height: 3'07"
Weight: 72.8 lbs.
Type: Dark

Trainers in Alola adore Persian for its coat, which is very smooth and has a velvety texture. This Pokémon has developed a haughty attitude and prefers to fight dirty when it gets into battle.

RAICHU

Height: 2'07"
Weight: 66.1 lbs.
Type: Electric

Raichu can unleash enough electricity to defeat a much larger Pokémon in a single devastating shock. When it's all charged up, it will attack just about anything—including its Trainer!

RATICATE

Height: 2'04"
Weight: 40.8 lbs.
Type: Normal

The webbing on its hind feet makes Raticate a good swimmer. Approach with caution—this Pokémon has a nasty temper and will bite with little provocation.

ALOLAN RAICHU

Height: 2'04"
Weight: 46.3 lbs.
Type: Electric-Psychic

Researchers speculate that Raichu looks different in the Alola region because of what it eats. It can "surf" on its own tail, standing on the flat surface and using psychic power to raise itself off the ground.

ALOLAN RATICATE

Height: 2'04"
Weight: 56.2 lbs.
Type: Dark-Normal

Each Raticate leads a group of Rattata, and the groups regularly scuffle over food. This Pokémon is rather picky about what it eats, so a restaurant where a Raticate lives is likely to be a good one.

RATTATA

Height: 1'00"
Weight: 7.7 lbs.
Type: Normal

Rattata's teeth keep growing throughout its life, so it has to chew on hard objects to keep them whittled down. They can live happily even in filthy conditions, which sometimes leads to overpopulation.

ALOLAN RATTATA

Height: 1'00"
Weight: 8.4 lbs.
Type: Dark-Normal

Rattata sleep during the day and spend their nights searching for the best food to bring back to the Raticate who leads them. They use their strong teeth to gnaw their way into people's kitchens.

SANDSHREW

Height: 2'00"
Weight: 26.5 lbs.
Type: Ground

Sandshrew often lives in the desert and other dry places, so it's accustomed to life with very little rainfall. It can move quickly by curling itself into a ball and rolling across the sand.

SANDSLASH

Height: 3'03"
Weight: 65.0 lbs.
Type: Ground

The spikes that cover Sandslash are sharp but brittle, easily broken on impact. Fortunately, they grow back very quickly. It sometimes ambushes foes by rolling up into a spiny ball and dropping from above.

ALOLAN SANDSHREW

Height: 2'04"
Weight: 88.2 lbs.
Type: Ice-Steel

Sandshrew lives high in the snowy mountains of Alola, where it has developed a shell of thick steel. It's very good at sliding across the ice—whether it does so under its own power or as part of a Sandshrew-sliding contest!

ALOLAN SANDSLASH

Height: 3'11"
Weight: 121.3 lbs.
Type: Ice-Steel

Sandslash is covered in spikes of tough steel, and in the cold mountains where it lives, each spike develops a thick coating of ice. A plume of snow flies up behind it as it dashes across the snowfield.

VULPIX

Height: 2'00"
Weight: 21.8 lbs.
Type: Fire

Vulpix is prized for its lovely
fur and multiple tails, which
keep splitting as it grows. Some
people think the ghostly fire from
its mouth is a departed spirit.

ALOLAN VULPIX

Height: 2'00"
Weight: 21.8 lbs.
Type: Ice

Vulpix in the Alola
region were
once known as
Keokeo, and
some older
folks still
use that name.
Its six tails can
create a spray of
ice crystals to cool
itself off when it
gets too hot.

TAPU KOKO

The Land Spirit Pokémon
How to say it: TAH-poo KO-ko
Height: 5'11"
Weight: 45.2 lbs.
Type: Electric–Fairy

Somewhat lacking in attention span, Tapu Koko is quick to anger but just as quickly forgets why it's angry. Calling thunderclouds lets it store up lightning as energy. It's known as the guardian of Melemele Island.

Tapu Koko took a special interest in Ash and Pikachu. It gave Ash a Z-Ring and then wanted to battle Ash. When Ash used his first Z-Move, Gigavolt Havoc, Pikachu unleashed an astonishingly powerful burst of electricity and then Ash's Z-Crystal shattered. But the experience just made Ash more determined to undergo an Island Challenge and earn a new Z-Crystal.

Z-RINGS

Professor Kukui has been teaching Ash all about what makes for an amazing Z-Move. First, a Trainer needs a Z-Ring, a band made of square metal plates. In the center of the Z-ring lies a large plate that holds the Z-Crystal. But this key tool isn't all a Trainer needs to use a Z-move.

The Z-Crystal and Z-Ring are powered by heart. A Pokémon and its Trainer must share a bond so strong that the Z-Ring can transform their feelings into power. However, their battle goals cannot be selfish. They must be fighting for something bigger than themselves—like helping the islands, helping Pokémon, or helping others. Only those who truly care about all living things in our world are permitted to use Z-Moves.

Kiawe earned his Z-Ring in a ceremony called the Island Challenge. Ash's first Z-Ring was a present from the guardian of Melemele Island, Tapu Koko. He earned his second Z-Crystal after completing an Island Challenge under the watchful eye of the island kahuna, Hala.

THE ISLAND KAHUNA

Every island in Alola has its own kahuna. In order to participate in the Island Challenge, Trainers need to seek the permission of the island kahuna. If the island kahuna decides that the Pokémon Trainer is worthy enough, it will assign a trial for the Trainer to complete. Only the island kahuna can decide if the Trainer has passed or failed the trial challenge.

If a Trainer proves him or herself and passes the first trial, the next step is the island's grand trial—battling the big kahuna himself.

THE ISLAND CHALLENGE

The Island Challenge is the kind of trial that tests a Trainer and teaches his or her skills to be stronger in battle. The kahuna of Melemele Island, Hala, explained to Ash that the challenge's true purpose is to give young people an appreciation for Alola's natural wonder. A Trainer wins the challenge when he or she recognizes how important it is to protect the islands on behalf of the many people and Pokémon who call Alola home.

Before Ash was permitted to participate in the first trial, Hala asked him a question to see if he had what it took to go through the actual trial itself. When Ash came back with the right answer, Hala gave him permission to participate.

For his trial, Ash battled Totem Pokémon to gain its help in chasing Rattata and Raticate away. But first, he and Pikachu went with Kahuna Hala to a pre-battle ceremony at the Ruins of Conflict. There they asked Tapu Koko to bestow the power of Alola of all the islands upon them.

Ash and Pikachu gave it their all in the battle against Hala and Hariyama—and they won!

ASH AND THE ISLAND CHALLENGE

Tapu Koko, the guardian of Melemele Island, took an interest in Ash almost from the very beginning of the young Trainer's vacation in Alola. Unbeknownst to Ash, it had been tracking him throughout his time in Alola.

One night during dinner, a cry echoed across the city. When Ash spotted Tapu Koko, he took off in search of it.

Tapu Koko led Ash and Pikachu to a lookout high above the city. Ash was awestruck. "Wow, the spirit guardian. It's Tapu Koko! Why do you keep coming to me?" he asked. "Is there something you want to tell me?"

Tapu Koko sparkled as it floated in the night sky above Ash and Pikachu. Then it released a glowing object that floated down to Ash.

"What's that?" asked Ash, holding out his hand. He took hold of the special, shiny band—the Z-Ring—and a flash of golden light burst from it. As Ash clicked the Z-Ring into place on his arm, he was completely absorbed by the bright light. Without another sound, Tapu Koko disappeared as quickly as it arrived.

The next day—Ash's first day at the Pokémon School—his new friends noticed the Z-Ring.

"That's so cool!" cried Sophocles.

"Whoa, Ash, is that a Z-Crystal on your wrist?" asked Mallow.

Kiawe went over for a closer look. "Yeah. It's an Electrium Z," he answered. "Where did you get that? Not the Island Challenge. You didn't participate and pass the trials that I know of."

"Tapu Koko gave it to me," Ash replied.

"No way!" exclaimed his new friends.

Ash explained how he met Tapu Koko the night before.

"Tapu Koko?" asked Kiawe. "How could it have gotten a Z-Ring?"

"It felt like Tapu Koko was telling me that the ring was for me," said Ash.

"I read about Tapu Koko before," added Lillie. "Tapu Koko's well known as the guardian who likes to help islanders, but it also likes to play tricks on people. And if it thinks it's necessary, it can sometimes even punish them. I also read that on rare occasions it will give mysterious gifts to people it likes."

"That's great!" Mallow cried. "Tapu Koko must really like Ash!"

"Kiawe, hold on," interrupted Sophocles. "You got your Z-Ring from the Akala Island kahuna, right?"

"Yeah," Kiawe said. "By successfully passing the grand trial."

"That's awesome," cheered Ash. "Does this mean I can use Z-Moves like you?"

"Z-Moves should not be taken lightly," warned Kiawe. "Only when a Pokémon's and its Trainer's hearts become one will the Z-Ring turn their feelings into power. But those feelings must be about something greater than themselves. Like helping the islands, helping Pokémon, or helping others. Only those who care about all living things in our world are permitted to use Z-Moves. I'm not exactly sure what Tapu Koko saw in you, but as a Z-Ring

owner, you need to realize your responsibility."

"Kiawe," Ash said. "I don't understand much of that complicated stuff, but I know how special the Z-Moves are. You can count on me."

"That's good enough," said Kiawe with a laugh.

The next day, the students at the Pokémon School threw Ash a surprise welcome party with some fun and challenging games. But halfway through the party, Tapu Koko made a surprise appearance!

Tapu Koko wanted to battle Ash and Pikachu. And it wanted them to try out their very first Z-Move, Gigavolt Havoc. As Pikachu unleashed an astonishingly powerful burst of electricity, Ash's Z-Crystal shattered.

Not one to give up easily, Ash decided it was time for him to enter an Island Challenge to earn a new Z-Crystal. To begin his trial, Ash first needed to visit Hala, the kahuna of Melemele Island.

No one had told him, but Hala already knew that Ash was on his way. Hala was waiting for Ash and had a challenge for him.

"I assume you now know that the people of this island have been troubled by a rash of wild Rattata and Raticate. If you were the person being asked to solve this problem, what would you do?" asked Hala.

"I know! I'd take Pikachu and Rowlet and challenge them all to a battle," began Ash.

"My young Ash," interrupted Hala. "Are you interested in learning why the Island Challenge was started so many years ago? You see, it wasn't simply to make Trainers stronger in battle. It was to raise young people in such a way that they will love and protect the islands of Alola as well as the people and Pokémon who inhabit them. I want you to look for answers that

won't only lead you to battle. We'll talk about the Z-Crystal after I've heard what you come up with."

Ash went back home and spent many hours trying to think of a way to solve the problem. When his classmates Mallow, Lana, Kiawe, Sophocles, and Lillie heard that Ash was having a hard time coming up with an answer, they offered to help him out. Brainstorming together with Rotom Dex, they came up with a brilliant strategy. They decided that recruiting Rattata and Raticate's natural rivals, Yungoos and Gumshoos, to chase them off would be the best solution.

Hala was pleased that Ash had come to this wise conclusion. Together he and Ash headed off to locate the enormous Totem Gumshoos and its allies to gain their assistance.

"There are several Yungoos and Gumshoos living in this cave," began Hala. "They are all very strong, but there is one Gumshoos that is amazingly powerful. It is called the Totem Pokémon."

"Totem Pokémon?" asked Ash.

"Yes," explained Hala. "There are several Pokémon in Alola who have that name. Most of them are following the lead of the Island Guardian as they assist Trainers who undertake the Island Challenge. So, Ash, your trial is to take on the Totem Pokémon in battle. Then, with the aid of the Totem Pokémon, I want you to chase away the Rattata and Raticate."

"But wait!" cried Ash, running into the cave after Hala. "Why would Gumshoos team up with me?"

"Never fear!" reassured Hala. "If you can earn the Totem Pokémon's respect

during your battle challenge, it will assist you in your time of need. I will be watching. I will be the referee during your trial."

Once inside the center of the huge cave, Hala called out to the Totem Pokémon, "Totem Pokémon Gumshoos! You have a trial goer! Do your duty and grant him his trial!"

Ash cried out, "I'm Ash Ketchum from Pallet Town! I'm asking you for a battle!"

The Totem Gumshoos' allies accepted Ash's challenge. So Ash called on his Pokémon pals Rowlet and Pikachu. With Pikachu's incredible Iron Tail and Rowlet's tough Tackle take down, Ash quickly defeated Totem Gumshoos' allies.

"Yungoos and Gumshoos are unable to battle," declared Hala.

Ash's celebration was short-lived. A thunderous roar echoed through the cave, and an enormous Gumshoos flew out at them.

"There!" declared Hala. "This Gumshoos is truly a Totem Pokémon!"

"It's so BIG!" cried Ash.

The impressive Totem Pokémon was too fast for its challengers. Rowlet quickly became exhausted, so Ash asked it to return. But just when it looked like Ash would be easily overpowered, he used his brainpower. Ash suggested Pikachu use a creative combination—Sand Attack to hide and then leap out and shock the Totem Pokémon with Thunderbolt.

Zap! The Totem Pokémon was left unable to battle.

Ash had won the round and the respect of the giant Totem Pokémon! Then Ash asked for its help. The Totem Pokémon agreed to go into town to get rid of all of the pests—and it also gave Ash a powerful and precious Z-Crystal.

Hala was very impressed. "For a Totem Pokémon to give a challenger a Z-Crystal is a very rare thing," he said to himself. "There's no doubt Ash must be a most unusual boy."

But his Island Challenge wasn't over yet. Next, Ash would have a grand trial—a battle against Kahuna Hala!

Ash again called on his Pokémon friend Rowlet to face off against Kahuna Hala and his Pokémon buddy Crabrawler, the Boxing Pokémon. Their battle was long and heated, but Rowlet used Tackle for the win.

Hala called on a force to be reckoned with—the Fighting-type Pokémon Hariyama. Ash chose his best buddy, Pikachu, but even its Thunderbolt had no effect on super-strong Hariyama. Especially when Hala unleashed the Fighting-type Z-Move, All-Out Pummeling.

But thanks to Quick Attack, Pikachu dodged every hit. Then, with one blow of Z-Move, Breakneck Blitz, Hariyama was left unable to battle. Pikachu and Ash had won the grand trial!

Hala intended to give Ash the Z-Crystal he favored, Fightinium Z, but Tapu Koko swooped in and replaced it with an Electrium Z.

"Fascinating!" exclaimed Hala. "This is the first time Tapu Koko has taken so much interest in a challenger. Eventually, I'll learn why. For now, I believe that this Electrium Z belongs to you. Take this Z-Crystal and use it with wisdom!"

"I will," promised Ash.

AMAZING BATTLES IN ALOLA

Ash and his friends have had some pretty cool battles in Alola. Here are some of the highlights.

ASH AND KIAWE VS. TEAM SKULL

Team Skull may have started this battle, but they were no match for their opponents, Ash and Kiawe. Together Ash, Pikachu, Kiawe, and Turtonator stood up to Salandit, Yungoos, and Zubat. Then Kiawe and Turtonator unleashed the Z-Move Inferno Overdrive to finish them off with a big, fiery explosion.

ASH VS. TAPU KOKO

Keen to see Ash in action with his new Z-Ring, Tapu Koko challenged our hero to a battle. But Ash was no match for the powerful Island Guardian. Ash tried his Gigavolt Havoc Z-Move. A blast of bright golden light burst across the sky toward Tapu Koko, but the Legendary Pokémon remained untouched. Unfortunately, Ash's Z-Crystal took the hit pretty hard—it completely disintegrated.

TEAM ROCKET VS. MIMIKYU

When Team Rocket arrived in Alola, they dreamed of capturing Mimikyu. But this dream soon turned into a nightmare! When Meowth jumped on Mimikyu and lifted its mask, it released a scary black cloud that sent Meowth down a long, dark tunnel. Luckily for Meowth, Jesse and James shook it awake. When Ash and his friends showed up and tried to capture Mimikyu, it decided to take sides . . . and it picked Team Rocket!

ASH AND SOPHOCLES VS. TEAM ROCKET

Atop the mall roof, Ash and Sophocles came face-to-face with Team Rocket and their newest member, Mimikyu, who was proving to be quite the challenger. Mimikyu sent Pikachu flying off the roof. But then Togedemaru harnessed the electricity from Pikachu's Thunderbolt to power up Zing Zap and turn into a ball of light. With one direct hit, it defeated Team Rocket.

ASH VS. HOBBES

Ash couldn't believe how lucky Lillie was to have a Pokémon battlefield right in her backyard! Ash and Rowlet seized the opportunity to challenge her butler, Hobbes, and his Pokémon pal, Oricorio. Rowlet tried a swirling Leafage storm, but it was no match for Oricorio's electric Revelation Dance. Next, Ash asked Rowlet to try Tackle. Rowlet cleverly mirrored Oricorio's Mirror Move, and the snap back sent Oricorio flying. But Oricorio's Double Slap proved to be too strong for Rowlet.

ASH VS. GUMSHOOS, THE TOTEM POKÉMON

The Totem Pokémon, Gumshoos, was gigantic and amazingly fast! Ash used Rowlet and Pikachu to battle the mighty Pokémon. In the end, Ash commanded Pikachu to use Sand Attack to hide until the Totem Pokémon got confused and collapsed. Then Pikachu finished the round with Thunderbolt. With this win, Ash won the first trial and earned the chance to battle Hala in the grand trial!

ASH VS. HALA

Ash faced off against Kahuna Hala in his first grand trial. Round one featured Ash and Rowlet against Hala and his Pokémon buddy Crabrawler. Although Rowlet sealed a win, it was so tired from the epic fight that it fell asleep in midair! Next, Hala chose the powerful Pokémon Hariyama, and Ash called on his best friend, Pikachu. Hala unleashed the Fighting-type Z-Move, All-Out Pummeling—but thanks to Quick Attack, Pikachu dodged every hit. Then Ash used the Z-Move Breakneck Blitz to win the grand trial!

ASH AND KIAWE VS. TEAM SKULL

Ash was excited for the chance to visit Akala Island and help his friend Kiawe with his Moomoo Milk deliveries. But just like Moomoo Milk, revenge is best served cold—and Team Skull was there to dish it out. The vile trio showed up and threatened to steal their precious cargo. So Ash and Pikachu stepped in and chased them off with a powerful punch of the Z-Move Gigavolt Havoc.

ALOLA FOR NOW!

What started as a short vacation to Alola has turned into an unforgettable adventure! Ash and Pikachu have made so many friends, met so many new species of Pokémon, and learned so much at the super-cool Pokémon School. The Trainer has taken his training to the next level. He's earned a Z-Ring and Z-Crystals, and he's learning to master Z-Moves.

Ash is just beginning to explore Alola. There's so much more to see and do! As he and Pikachu continue to travel through the island paradise, more action-packed battles and surprises await them. But one thing is certain—Ash's journey through the Alola region has brought him one step closer to his dream of becoming a Pokémon Master!